001325118

Jackson County Li...
Medford, OR 97501

Eagle
Point

D0395737

DATE DUE			▶ 3/01
MAY 25 0			
JUN 24 '02			
MAY 14 '04			
GAYLORD			PRINTED IN U.S.A.

AN
ORCA
YOUNG
READER

Three on Three

ERIC WALTERS

ORCA BOOK PUBLISHERS

JACKSON COUNTY LIBRARY SERVICES
MEDFORD OREGON 97501

Copyright © 1999 Eric Walters

No part of this book may be reproduced, stored in a retrieval system, or transmitted, in any form or by any means, without the prior written permission of the publisher, except by a reviewer who may quote brief passages in review.

Canadian Cataloguing in Publication Data
Walters, Eric, 1957–
Three on three

ISBN 1-55143-170-X

I. Title.
PS8595.A598T57 1999   jC813'.54   C99-910904-9
PZ7.W17129Th 1999

Library of Congress Catalog Card Number: 99-65484

Orca Book Publishers gratefully acknowledges the support of our publishing programs provided by the following agencies: the Department of Canadian Heritage, The Canada Council for the Arts, and the British Columbia Arts Council.

Cover design by Christine Toller
Cover illustration by John Mantha
Interior illustrations by Kirsti

IN CANADA	IN THE UNITED STATES
Orca Book Publishers	Orca Book Publishers
PO Box 5626, Station B	PO Box 468
Victoria, BC Canada	Custer, WA USA
V8R 6S4	98240-0468

01 00 99   5   4   3

Printed in Canada

*With apologies to Kyle,
and thanks to Kia.*

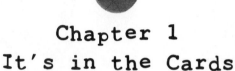

Chapter 1
It's in the Cards

"Come on everybody, let's get in and start working," Mrs. Orr said, before ducking into the room.

Kids began hanging up their coats and backpacks and shuffling into the classroom.

"Nick, have a look at this," Kia said as she pulled something out of the pocket of her jacket.

"Wow! It's a Julius 'The Jewel' Johnson basketball card! Where did you get it?"

"I spent all my birthday money on cards

last night," Kia grinned.

"All your money?"

"Every cent I had."

"And your mother said you could?" I couldn't believe it.

There was a pause. "Well, she didn't say yes," Kia admitted, "but she didn't say no either."

I gave her a confused look. "So what you're saying is … ?"

"She doesn't exactly *know* I bought them. And she never will, unless she counts my cards and finds out I have two hundred and eighty-one instead of one hundred and ninety-two," she explained, pulling out a hand full of cards from her other pocket.

"But if she does find out, she'll kill you."

"No she won't. She said I couldn't just waste my money. I had to save it for something special."

"Yeah … your point?"

"Can you think of anything more special than basketball cards?"

I thought for a second. The only person I knew who liked b-ball more than Kia was me. "You're right, nothing is more special than basketball cards ... especially a Julius 'The Jewel' Johnson card."

"Are you two waiting for a special invitation to come into class?' Mrs. Orr asked in an annoyed voice.

"Um ... no ...," I stammered, realizing that aside from our teacher, Kia and I were the only two people left in the hall.

"Hurry up!" she said and then she popped back into the class.

I took another look at the Julius Johnson card. It showed him driving for the basket, suspended in mid-flight. He was the greatest player around — my hero — the guy I always pretended to be when I was playing basketball. I tried to cross-over dribble the ball the way he did. I made sure I got his number on my basketball jersey. I left the back of my shirt untucked the way 'The Jewel' did. I even wanted to have my hair done exactly the same way he wore his — and I would have, if my mother didn't think it was wrong for a ten-year-old to have his hair dyed green and blue.

Reluctantly I handed the card back to Kia. We hurried into the class just as the national anthem came crackling out of the P.A. I snapped to attention, my hands at my sides, my head held high, and sang out all the words.

Without even looking over, I knew Kia was standing the same way, and could hear her singing just as loud. Mrs. Orr often commented on how much respect we showed. She once even sent in a little slip of paper to the office and our names were read during the announcements as 'Clark Boulevard Public School All-Stars' for the way we stood so still and sang so strong.

What Mrs. Orr didn't know was that, when the national anthem played, we pretended we were standing center court in front of seventeen thousand people, waiting for the game to start. After all, it was important for superstars like us to set a good example for our loyal fans. That was our shared fantasy. Me to be in the NBA, and Kia to be in the WNBA — the Women's National Basketball Association. Kia was just about the best athlete in all of Grade Three. She was taller than all the boys, as strong as most of them, and could out-play them at just about any sport you could name.

The anthem ended and Kia and I gave each other a slight nod of the head. We went and joined the rest of the class sitting on the carpet. Kia sat at one side, with the rest of the girls, and I sat on the other, with the boys.

Sometimes it wasn't easy for either of us to be friends. Kids were always making some joke or comment about us 'liking' each other. Of course we liked each other ... but not *that* way. When we were in kindergarten, it was okay for girls and boys to hang out together, but with each passing year it was getting harder. So to make things a little bit easier, we agreed not to talk to each other while we were in class. After announcements, Mrs. Orr asked, "Whose turn is it to lead the opening exercises?"

"It's mine," Tim said, rising to his feet. He shuffled through the bodies on the carpet until he got to the blackboard. He picked up the pointer and put the tip on our class motto.

"Positive people in Room Two respect everybody. We cooperate and learn," the class read out together, following Tim as he pushed the pointer from word to word.

"Good work, Tim. We'll start today with page seventy-eight in the math book, and then ... Kia what are you playing with?"

I knew without looking over what it was.

"My new cards," Kia said.

"I know I've spoken to you before about bringing cards to the carpet. I also know this is going to be the very last time I'm going to need to mention it."

"The last time?" Kia asked nervously.

"Yes. Because the next time you play with cards during school time, I'm going to take them away from you … for good."

I gasped out loud.

Mrs. Orr turned to me. "You don't agree with that, Nicholas?"

She always called me 'Nicholas,' even though the rest of the world called me Nick. Nick would sound better when the announcer introduced me before the game. I could just see it — the crowd roaring — smoke and strobe lights flashing as the announcer screams out my name and I run onto the court and …

"Well, Nicholas?" she asked again.

I snapped back to reality. "Um … taking away her cards seems pretty tough, Mrs. Orr. Couldn't you just send her down to the office or suspend her or something?"

"Yeah, just send me to the office," Kia insisted, "that would be fair."

"Fair is keeping my word, and I'm going to keep my word. The next time I see those cards, they're mine, so put them away. Now!"

Kia scrambled to her feet and hurried out the door to put her cards safely in her backpack hanging in the hall. She quickly came back in and settled into her spot on the carpet among the other girls.

"And after everybody is finished with their math problems," Mrs. Orr continued, "I want you to do a journal entry."

Kia gave me a wink and I knew what she'd be writing about — her new cards.

"You can write about anything," Mrs. Orr continued, "except basketball."

"What, no basketball!" I protested, raising my hand. "But why?"

"Because some of you write about nothing *but* basketball."

I knew that 'some' of us meant Kia and me. I raised my hand again.

"Yes, Nicholas?"

"I've written about other things," I protested.

"You have? Like what?" Mrs. Orr asked.

I had to strain my mind to think. "Well ... I've written about playing video games, and going out with my father ... "

"And television too, watching TV," Kia added.

"As I remember, you both have written about those things," Mrs. Orr agreed.

Kia and I exchanged a smile.

"Written about playing basketball video games, and going out with your parents to a basketball game, and watching basketball on television," Mrs. Orr continued. "So today you're going to — "

A heavy knock on the door interrupted her. Two kids bounced to their feet to get it, but before they'd moved three steps, the door opened. Mr. Roberts, our gym teacher, poked his head in.

"Hi, Mrs. Orr. Can I borrow your kids for a couple of minutes?"

"I think we can spare the time."

The rest of him followed his head into the room. Like always he was dressed in a T-shirt and sweatpants. I wondered if he even owned other clothes. I could picture him getting married in his sweats ... maybe with a tie around his neck to make it more formal.

Carefully he picked his way through the class. As he passed, I drew my hands and feet in close to my body. He was really big — it would hurt to have him step on me. He stopped at the front of the class. It seemed strange to see him by a blackboard instead of in the gym.

"Good morning, boys and girls."

"Good morning, Mr. Roberts," we all parroted back.

Suddenly he leaped into the air and landed on top of Mrs. Orr's desk. My mouth dropped in disbelief and a gasp rose from the class.

"There, that's better," Mr. Roberts said. "An important announcement requires a stage."

My eyes couldn't help but be drawn to his feet, which almost at eye level. He was wearing a pair of brand new basketball shoes. The white and black stripes made them look like high-tech, high-top zebras.

"Nice shoes," I blurted out.

"Thanks, Nick. And interestingly, these shoes have to do with my announcement. I'm going around to all the grade three, four, and five classes this morning. You're all invited to enter the First Annual Clark Boulevard Three-on-Three Basketball Tournament."

Chapter 2
The Contest

The only thing louder than the cheer from the kids was the groan from Mrs. Orr.

Mr. Roberts raised a hand above his head, just like he did in gym class, to get our attention. Everybody fell silent. "Put up your hand if you like the game."

A sea of hands shot up into the air. I tried to get my hand higher than anybody else's, like I was reaching up for a tip-off.

"Good. Now most of the rules of three-on-three basketball are the same as regular ball. But there are only three people to a team, and both sides shoot for the same basket."

"When will it start?" Adam blurted out.

I glanced over at Mrs. Orr, who didn't seem pleased that Adam was just yelling out questions. Mr. Roberts didn't seem to notice or care.

"The contest will start next week," he began. "Each team will play five games and then the top eight teams will go on to the playoffs. Yes, Deidre?" he asked in answer to another raised hand.

"This isn't just for the boys, is it?"

"Of course not! Not only are some of the girls in this school excellent players …," he said, glancing in Kia's direction. She smiled in response. "… but all students naturally compete in all activities at this school. You are going to sign up aren't you, Deidre?"

Deidre nodded her head and practically beamed. She was a pretty good player, as was another one of the girls in the class, Nandinie, but neither was even close to Kia.

A buzz went up as people began to talk about who was going to play and who wasn't.

"Quiet down," Mr. Roberts said, "or I won't tell you about the prizes."

"Prizes!" a couple of kids screamed out before the rest of us 'shushed' them and they fell silent.

"Each member of the winning team will receive two tickets to the Air Canada Centre to see the Raptors play the Bulls … "

A gasp rose from the class.

" … and a basketball personally signed by Julius Johnson."

I had to stop myself from jumping to my feet. I looked over at Kia and her face mirrored what I felt. A ball signed by Johnson was about the only thing that could possibly be better than one of his cards.

I raised my hand and Mr. Roberts nodded in my direction. "Do we get to choose our own teams?"

"Yes you can choose your own teams, with some exceptions."

"Exceptions?" I asked. I knew there

would be some catch.

"Yes, because the contest is open to students in grades three through five, I've had to make a rule to level the playing field. No team can be made up of only grade five students. So those grade five students who wish to be part of the contest must find at least one other student in grade three or four to be part of the team."

That sounded like a very, very good exception.

"How many people are interested in entering the contest?" Mr. Roberts asked.

Most of the hands in the room shot up into the air. Kia had both hands held high.

"Excellent! To be eligible to enter the contest you must write a poem on basketball," Mr. Roberts said.

"We have to what?" I asked in disbelief.

"You're kidding, right, Mr. Roberts?" Kia asked.

Mr. Roberts was always joking around with us in gym. If you were late for class he'd ask if you'd been abducted by aliens or been in jail. He had to be kidding.

"I'm serious. Every member of each team must write a poem about basketball to enter the contest."

There was a stunned silence. What did writing a poem have to do with playing basketball? I could bet that nobody ever asked 'The Jewel' to write a poem!

"And it's not just poetry that will involve basketball," Mr. Roberts continued. "I've prepared a whole unit of study where everything — story writing, journal entries, even math — will involve basketball." He leapt off the desk and his voice became even more animated. "I'd like kids to go on the 'Net and search out basketball web sites. I've got a list of e-mail addresses for some of your favorite players if you want to write them. You can find basketball novels — I've set up a whole shelf in the library. I want you to think of basketball as not just a game, but a way of life! Do you think you can do that?"

"I think I can manage!" I shot back, supported by cheers from Kia and the other kids.

"Of course, you can only do all the basketball-related themes if it's okay with your teacher," Mr. Roberts said.

The room fell silent and all eyes turned to Mrs. Orr. We were dead. This was the teacher who had just, seconds before, told us she was sick of reading about basketball, and now it was all up to her.

"Most of the other teachers have agreed to it," Mr. Roberts said encouragingly.

"Have they?" Mrs. Orr asked.

"Most of them."

Mrs. Orr cleared her throat and very slowly looked around the room. I held my breath and said a silent prayer.

"I think," Mrs. Orr said, "that would be all right."

Kids cheered. I felt like screaming, like laughing, like jumping up and running around the room, even like giving Mrs. Orr a hug — but I didn't. Instead I looked over at Kia and she was looking at me.

And I knew that she was thinking the same thing as me — who would we choose as the third member of our team?

Chapter 3
The Draft

We were excited after Mr. Roberts left, but Mrs. Orr got us down to work really quickly. The whole thing seemed like a dream. Imagine — I was going to enter a basketball contest, win prizes and even write about basketball at school. The only bad part was the poem. Poetry was majorly stupid, but what could I do?

I looked up at the clock. It was only a few minutes until recess. I hurried to finish my journal entry before the bell went. If it wasn't finished I'd have to stay in and finish it — that was Mrs. Orr's rule.

I wrote about winning the contest, and how I'd put that ball in a place of honor. Maybe my Dad would even build a special case for it. He'd do that for something that important — especially if it involved basketball.

I was on the last sentence of my entry when the recess bell rang. I scribbled the final few words.

"All those who have handed in their journal entries are free to go to out for recess," Mrs. Orr said.

As the kids headed for the door, I fought my way upstream to Mrs. Orr's desk and tossed my journal onto the pile of other books.

Kia was waiting for me in the hall, holding a tennis ball. "Wanna play foot hockey?" she asked.

"Of course not. We have to get a third player and then practice!"

She shrugged. "What's the point? It's not like we're going to win or anything."

"What are you talking about?" I demanded. "Of course we can win! We're the two best players in grade three!"

"Maybe, but aren't you forgetting a couple of things?" Kia asked.

"I am? Like what?"

"Grades four and five."

Her words hit me like a slap in the face. What was I thinking … or I guess, what wasn't I thinking? How could I forget about almost one hundred kids — all of them older, most of them bigger, and some of them better at the game then either me or Kia.

I slipped on my coat as the dream slipped away. Of course she was right. Sometimes at recess I'd stand off to the side and watch the grade fives play basketball. They never allowed us 'little kids' into the game. If they'd let me or Kia play, we could have beaten most of them. But not all. Some were pretty good, and there were two — Marcus and Kingsley — who were really, really good. Of the two, Marcus was the best. I'd seen him play in the community center gym where his team often had games scheduled right after ours.

Well, next year those guys would be gone from our school. I'd just have to wait for the Second Annual Clark Boulevard Public School Three-on-Three contest.

"I guess we should still enter the contest anyway," Kia said.

I shrugged. "It'll be fun, even if we don't win. Any ideas who we should get for the third player?"

"I don't know. Maybe Kyle or Paul or…" Kia stopped and a smile came to her face. "Or Marcus."

"Marcus!" I yelped. "What makes you think he'll play with us?"

"Don't you remember what Mr. Roberts said? There can't be three grade fives on a team. He might just be looking for a team. It can't really hurt to ask him. Besides, didn't you tell me that he once talked to you?"

"Um … he didn't really talk to me … he sort of talked about me."

"What did he say about you?" Kia asked.

"I couldn't hear it all," I admitted reluctantly. "But it was something like, 'let the kid out of the garbage can.'"

"What?" Kia asked.

"Let the kid out of the garbage can."

She laughed. "Why would he say that?"

"Because I was in a garbage can."

"What were you doing in a garbage can?"

"I climbed in," I answered meekly.

"You climbed in? Why would you do that?"

"Because three bigger kids told me I had a choice. Either I could climb in or they'd stuff me in. I figured climbing in would hurt less than being stuffed."

"When did this happen?" Kia asked.

"About a year ago."

"But ... but, why?"

"Do older kids ever need a reason to pick on younger kids? They said I crossed over the basketball court while they were playing and it wasn't safe to leave garbage lying on the ground in case somebody stepped on it."

"Did they let you out when Marcus told them to?"

"Sort of. They knocked the can on its side and then rolled it down the little hill beside the court."

Kia began to chuckle and I remembered clearly why I never told her any of this before.

I frowned. "Glad you think it was funny. I was dizzy for ten minutes and picked garbage out of my hair and pockets for an hour after that. And I *still* think my jacket smells like squashed bananas."

"So," Kia said, "Marcus not only knows you, but he even helped you. Come on, let's go and ask him before he joins up with somebody else."

Kia set off across the playground toward the basketball court and I reluctantly trailed after her. I didn't think there was much point in asking him, but I knew there was absolutely no point in trying to talk her out of it. Once Kia got an idea in her head, she didn't like being confused with the facts.

When we arrived, there were two games going on. At one hoop there were a few people playing. Around the other net a small crowd had gathered to watch, and I figured that would be where Marcus was playing. Kia and I took a spot at the edge of the semicircle of kids observing the action.

Marcus was on the court along with a bunch of grade five kids. They were playing a game of four-on-four. Aside from Marcus, who was clearly the best, a couple of the other players were pretty good. The rest were just big, stumbling and bumping into each other. It looked more like they were playing football or hockey.

I took my eyes off the game and looked at the crowd. Without exception, every kid standing around us was in grade five. And almost all of them were from the complex.

The complex was a gigantic apartment building a few blocks away from the school. The kids from there were different from the rest of us who lived in the homes surrounding the school. Most of those kids were tougher and didn't seem to mind getting in trouble, or at least had more practice at it.

I leaned in close to Kia. "Let's get out of here," I said under my breath. "This isn't a safe place for a grade three to be. These guys are all in grade five, and most of them are from the complex."

She shrugged and nodded her head. Even Kia had lost her nerve.

We began to walk away when the ball clanked noisily off the ring, bounced wildly and landed right in my hands. Everybody was looking right at me. It was too late to pretend to be invisible.

"Give me the ball!" demanded one of the kids, as he walked toward me menacingly.

I looked at the ball, then I looked at him. Just as he reached out for the ball, I did a cross-over dribble, sidestepped him, jumped into the air and launched the ball for the net.

Chapter 4
Swoosh!

The ball floated through the air in a perfect arch … up, up, up and then down, down, down and …

SWOOSH! Right into the hoop, nothing but net.

"Nice shot!" Kia yelled.

"Lucky shot, don't you mean?" the kid I'd sidestepped said. He walked past me and back towards the action.

"Nope," I corrected him. "You'd have been lucky to stop me."

He turned around and glared at me. Instantly I knew I should have kept my mouth buttoned. Trash talk could get a guy put in a garbage can.

"What did you say?" he demanded.

"Nothing," I mumbled.

A kid on the sidelines chipped in, "He said you'd have been lucky to stop him."

"Give the little punk the ball! I wasn't ready. I'd like to see him do it again."

"Come on, Roy," Marcus called out, "we haven't got time for this." He was holding the basketball.

I'd heard about Roy. He'd just transferred to the school last week and already he'd been in trouble a lot, including a fight. This was getting worse by the second.

"Recess is more than half over and I'm still not sure who's good enough to be on my team," Marcus continued.

So that's what this is, I thought. A tryout to see who got to be on Marcus' team for the tournament.

"This will only take a second," Roy said. "Besides, this can be part of my tryout."

Marcus bounced the ball a few times and looked at me. Then, without saying another word, he whistled a chest pass so strong I stumbled backwards as I caught it. Kids all around chuckled.

"Okay," Roy demanded, "let's see your stuff, you little geek."

I squeezed the ball tightly in my hands. Whether I got a basket or not, I knew I was going to lose. Roy scowled at me angrily and the kids behind me began to jeer. I took a deep breath and bounced the ball nervously. Roy lunged forward. Instinctively I fed the ball through my legs and cut around him to the left, leaving him grabbing for air. I broke for the basket, but I was hit hard from behind. The ball squirted loose.

"Foul!" Marcus cried.

"Foul? I hardly touched him!" Roy screamed and walked right up to Marcus. Marcus was big, but Roy was even bigger. They stood eyeball to eyeball.

"Okay, it wasn't a foul," Marcus said.

"That's right, no foul," Roy chuckled.

"But it was out off of you. It's Nick's ball."

I don't know what surprised me more, the fact that it was my ball or that Marcus knew my name. Somebody handed Marcus the ball and he lobbed it gently to me.

"Take it out again from the top of the key," he said.

I slowly walked back. The crowd surrounding the court was now much, much bigger. It looked like most of the grade fives, as well as lots of kids from the other grades, were crowding in on all sides. It reminded me of the way people gathered whenever a fight started. Oh, great.

"Come on, Nick, you can take him!" called out a voice.

I smiled weakly. What I *didn't* need was kids taunting Roy and getting him even madder. He gave me a look which could only be described as scary. The crowd pushed in from behind. Roy stood in front of me. There was no way out and — even worse, no way to win.

I began dribbling the ball. This time he

didn't charge forward. He stood there, crouched over, and glared at me. I faked in and back out, and he reached forward. He missed the ball but slapped me in the arm.

"That was no foul!" Roy screamed.

I switched the ball to my left hand and turned my body to protect it. This way there was less chance of him taking a swipe at the ball and hitting me instead. Maybe if I just kept on dribbling, I could wait him out and the bell would ring.

Smack!

My arm stung where he'd slapped me again. This time he didn't even bother to say anything. He smirked and then jumped forward. I spun to my right, swerved by him, bounced the ball through my legs to the right hand and drove for the open basket.

"Ugggh!" I grunted as I was driven into the pavement. He'd tackled me and his arms were wrapped around my legs.

"Stupid little …," he began.

"What's going on here?" called out an adult voice. Ms. Carberry pushed through the crowd.

Roy let go of my legs and quickly got to his feet.

"What's going on here?" the teacher demanded again.

"Nothing," Roy blurted out. "Nothing at all. We were playing basketball and this kid fell over his own feet. That's all."

Ms. Carberry looked at Roy suspiciously and then at me. "Is that what happened Nick?"

I didn't answer.

"Is it?"

Nothing was worse than a snitch. Especially a dead snitch. I nodded my head. I struggled to my feet and my knee hurt. I looked down. My pants were ripped and blood was coming out of the tear.

Ms. Carberry frowned. "Nick, you're hurt! Go to the office and get it looked at. Kia, you go with him … and Marcus you go along too."

"Me?" Marcus asked in surprise. "I didn't do anything!"

"I didn't say you did, but you're in grade five and should be responsible for helping the younger children."

"But the bell is going to ring in a few minutes and we still have to figure out who's going to … "

"Don't argue. Just go!" Ms. Carberry ordered him.

Marcus shook his head, but kept his mouth closed as he walked over to me.

Kia had picked up the ball when it had popped loose after I was tackled. She went to hand it to Marcus.

"It's not my ball. I don't want it," he said. "Shoot it."

"Shoot it?"

"Yeah, like a foul shot."

Kia faced the net and put up the ball. It hit the rim, hit the backboard, circled the rim again and dropped. The kids cheered.

Roy stepped toward me. "Boy, are you one unlucky kid."

"What do you mean unlucky?" I asked.

"You'll find out," he said with a scowl.

Chapter 5
The Team

"What did he mean by that?" I asked, as Kia and Marcus led me away to the office.

"He meant nothing," Marcus said. "Just talk."

"Are you sure?" I asked anxiously.

"Probably. Some nice moves out there."

"Thanks." Suddenly my knee didn't hurt as much.

"I guess you still need to make up your team for the three-on-three contest," Kia said.

"Yeah, I'll have to wait until next recess."

"You don't have to wait," Kia suggested.

Marcus looked puzzled.

"We came over because we were looking for a third person. Do you want to be on our team?"

"Your team!" he snorted.

"Yeah. What's so funny about that?" I asked.

"You're just little kids."

"Grade three's not that little. Besides, you said yourself that I have some good moves."

"You do have some moves," Marcus admitted. "And you can shoot and re-bound," he directed to Kia.

"Thanks ... how do you know I can rebound?"

"I've seen you both play before."

"You have? When?"

"A few weeks ago at the 'Y'. I was waiting for my team's practice to start so I watched a bit of your game. You're both pretty good ... about the best on the floor ... but that was against kids your own age."

"So why not join up with us?" Kia asked.

"You're good, but I can get partners who are better. I was thinking of me and Kingsley being on the same team."

"Kingsley's a great player!" Kia exclaimed.

"He's good," Marcus said with a shrug. "Probably the second best player in the school."

If the two of them were on the same side, they'd win no matter who else they picked for their team.

"And then we'll need a third player," Marcus said.

"Somebody in grade three or four," Kia said quickly.

"Yeah," Marcus admitted, "that's right."

We walked a few more feet when without warning Marcus grabbed my arm and spun me around. "Maybe I should have *you* on my team as the third person."

"Him?" Kia asked in a surprised tone.

For a split second I had a rush of excitement. I wouldn't have to wait for another year to field a winning team. Being on a team with Marcus and Kingsley would guarantee a win, guarantee a ticket to the game, and guarantee me an autographed basketball!

I looked over at Kia. Her face looked like a ball losing its air. If I said yes, I'd also guarantee one more thing — I'd hurt my best friend.

"Sorry," I answered. "I'm already on a team. But our team still has one more space open."

Kia beamed at me.

"You can join our team ... unless ...," I paused. I knew what I wanted to say, but I was afraid of how he'd react.

"Unless what?" Marcus asked.

"Nothing."

"Let's hear it," he demanded.

I swallowed hard. Either he'd bite on my suggestion or bite my head off. "Unless you're afraid that if you don't have Kingsley on your team you can't win."

"What? Are you saying he's better than me?" There was more than a hint of anger in his voice.

"Not me!" I said, holding my hands up. "I know you're better than him, but lots of kids — you know, kids who don't really know basketball — might think he's better than you."

"Well he's not!"

"We know that," Kia said, jumping in. "Anyway, I guess it's smarter to take the safe way out."

"What do you mean, safe?" Marcus asked.

Kia shrugged. "You know, with you and Kingsley on the same side, you don't have to be afraid of losing."

"What are you talking about?" Marcus asked.

"I know what she means," I said.

"What?" His voice was getting louder with each question.

"It's just ... just ..."

"Spit it out!"

I had a terrible fear that I might be spitting out teeth in a minute. He looked mad enough to take a swing at me.

I took a deep breath. "She means that some people only play when they know they're going to win. It isn't even a contest if you and Kingsley are on the same team."

"That's right," Kia agreed. "But if you played with us and we won, then everybody would see that you were the best player in the whole school."

"You couldn't lose!" I added. "Either we'd win — and I think we would if we practiced hard — and everybody would know you're the greatest, or we'd lose and it wouldn't be your fault because you had a couple of grade threes on your team."

Marcus shook his head and began to chuckle softly to himself.

"It would be something if I won with two little kids on my side. People would talk about it for sure."

"Especially the grade threes. Every grade three in the school would be cheering for us," I said.

"Not just the grade threes," Kia said. "The whole school would be on our side. Even the teachers! Everybody loves an underdog. You'd be like a hero!"

She was right. Everybody *would* be cheering for us. Nobody said another word as we walked into the office and up to the counter.

"What can I do for you three?" Mrs. Brown, the school secretary asked.

"He cut himself ... probably needs to have it cleaned up," Marcus said.

"We'll take care of him," Mrs. Brown replied reassuringly.

"Good. I wouldn't want anything bad to happen to one of my teammates."

"Teammates!" I exclaimed.

"That's what I said. Did you hurt your ears as well when you fell?"

Chapter 6
Home Court Advantage

I ran a finger down the list of teams entered in the contest. A check mark was beside the names of anybody who'd already written a poem. Most of the names were ticked off.

"Do you see it?" Kia asked.

I ignored her and kept looking. I found our team. Beside Kia's name and mine was a red check mark. We'd worked on our poems that first night and finished them up. My mother had let us use her rhyming dictionary, which listed all the words in the world that rhymed. It made it a lot easier.

"Well?" she asked. Nobody could ever accuse Kia of not being persistent.

"Nope, he hasn't written a poem."

"Maybe he's written it, but it just hasn't been marked off yet. Let's check with Mr. Roberts."

It seemed like a good idea. I trailed after Kia down the hall. Sometimes it seemed like I was always trailing after her. My Mom sometimes joked that learning to listen to Kia was good practice for marriage. I didn't think there was anything remotely funny about her saying those sort of things.

Kia knocked on the door of Mr. Roberts' office. Actually it was really more like a storage room for gym equipment, but he'd shoved in a desk and a CD player.

"Come!" a voice yelled through the closed door.

Kia pushed it open and music, which had been leaking out from under the closed door, flooded out into the hall, practically pushing us back. Mr. Roberts was sitting at his desk. His feet were up and he had a newspaper — the sports section — opened up in front of him. He turned down the music, and put down the paper.

"What can I do for you two?"

"We were wondering if you had Marcus' poem yet?" Kia asked.

"Is it marked off the list?"

"No."

"No mark, no poem."

"We were just thinking maybe you didn't have a chance to mark it," I explained. "We know how busy you are."

"Nope. You know tomorrow is the deadline. Without that poem your team can't enter the tournament."

We both nodded our heads. He wasn't telling us something that we didn't know already. Marcus had been promising us for a week that he'd have the poem finished.

"And it would be a shame if your team wasn't in it," he continued. "The three of you would give the other teams a good run."

"What do you mean a 'good run'?" I asked.

"A good game — some competition — you might even make it to the playoffs."

"*Might* reach the playoffs?!" Kia practically yelled. "We're going to win!"

Mr. Roberts smiled. "That's the attitude Kia, never give up!"

"It's not just an attitude. We're pretty good."

"I know that. You two are definitely the best players in grade three, and we all know about Marcus. But the three of you are giving up a lot of age and size to some of the other teams."

We couldn't argue with that. A bunch of the teams had two grade-five players and one kid from grade four.

"But I guess none of that matters much. If I don't have Marcus' poem in my hand by nine o'clock tomorrow, your team doesn't qualify."

"You'll have it, don't worry," I reassured him.

We only had a few minutes until the

bell. We hurried off to find Marcus. We were headed for the basketball nets when I spied him off in the field kicking around a soccer ball. As we approached him the bell rang and the game broke up.

"Hey, Marcus!" I called out.

He gave a weak wave and started off to the door where his class and the other grade fives lined up. We walked over to meet him.

"Mr. Roberts says you haven't handed in your poem yet," Kia said.

"Still working on it."

"It's due tomorrow," I added.

"I know the days of the week. I'll have it in by tomorrow."

"You've been saying that all week," Kia said.

"Who are you, a supply teacher?" Marcus snapped. "I said I'd do it and I will!"

"It's a stupid assignment," I offered. "It wasn't easy for us either. Do you want some help?"

"What sort of help?"

"I was just wondering if you maybe

wanted to come over to my place after school and we could work on it."

"Yeah, Nick is really good with poems and stuff," Kia added.

"Good with poems? You write poems?" I could tell by his voice he thought it was pretty funny.

"Not really. Just for school. But I have a special rhyming dictionary at home and it really helped. You want to come over?"

Marcus didn't answer.

"Come on," I suggested. "We can help you with the poem. Then maybe we can play a little ball, you know, get some practice in."

"Play some ball?" he asked. He seemed a little more interested.

"Yeah, we can use my new ball. It's official size and weight," Kia added.

"You have a hoop?" Marcus asked.

"In my driveway," I said.

Kia nodded. "He has the best court around. He's got one of those elevator poles that lets it go up or down. When it's low enough we can even dunk!"

"As long as we don't hang from the rim. My father said he'd string up anybody who hung from the rim."

"And the backboard is Plexiglas," Kia continued, "and best of all, the driveway is lined."

"What do you mean lined?" Marcus asked.

"The key and the three-point line are painted right there on the driveway."

"Are you kidding?"

"No," I answered, shaking my head.

"Sounds cool."

"So," I said, "are you coming over?"

"I'll think about it."

"Do you have to call somebody and ask?" Kyle said.

"Naw ... I'm on my own after school this week anyway. My old man is working twelve-hour day shifts this week so he doesn't get home until after seven — later if there's any overtime."

Kia frowned. "What about your mother?"

There was a pause. "There's nobody at home. I take care of myself."

"But what about supper?" Kia continued. That was like Kia to be worried about food.

"Sometimes I wait for my father, but most of the time I just fix myself something."

"You cook?" I asked.

"How hard is it to open a can of spaghetti?" He paused. "Is it okay for you to just bring somebody home? I'm not allowed anybody in when my father isn't there."

"My mother never minds an extra person around."

"I *hope* she doesn't mind," Kia said. "I'm there practically every day after school."

"Every day, huh?" Marcus asked. "Are you two like girlfriend and boyfrie—"

"No!" we both yelled, cutting him off.

"We're just friends," I said.

"Yeah, friends," Kia added.

"So are you coming over?" I asked, quickly changing the subject.

"Like I said, I'll think about it. If I decide to come, I'll meet you two at the swings right after the bell."

Chapter 7
Roses are Red

"You guys are late," Marcus said, jumping off the swing. "What took you so long? I was just getting ready to leave."

"Sorry," I apologized.

"Nick had to stay after school to finish up his work," Kia explained.

"Been there, done that," Marcus said.

Maybe it was something that had happened to Marcus before, but it was a first for me. I was so distracted wondering if he was going to show, I had trouble finishing my work.

We hurried out of the school yard and along the streets. It was important we make up for the time I'd lost finishing my work. My mother never minded me having friends come over, but she did mind me being late.

"That must be your place up ahead," Marcus said.

"Yeah ... how did you know?" I asked in surprise.

"The driveway has a court painted on it. Dead giveaway. This is probably the only driveway like that in the world. I'm surprised your father let you do it."

"Nick didn't do it," Kia said. "His father did."

"You're kidding."

"My father is crazy about sports. Of course, when he told my mother about his plan, she was pretty concerned."

"She doesn't like basketball?" Marcus asked.

"She thinks it's okay. She was just worried that if he didn't do it right, it would look awful. She likes things done the correct way, that's all."

As we walked up the driveway Marcus stopped, bent down and ran a hand along one of the lines. He looked up. "It looks *really* good. Are all the lines in the right places?"

"Yep. I helped my dad put them on. He measured them so they'd be perfect."

Marcus nodded. "Let's play some ball."

"Let's have a snack first," Kia suggested.

"And work on the poem," I added. "There's no point in practicing until we know we can play."

"We could write poetry and eat at the same time," Kia said. Typical Kia. But I had to admit that I was hungry too. I held open the door for them and we all entered the house.

"I'm home, Mom!" I bellowed as we all took off our shoes.

"Hi, honey!" Her voice came rolling down from upstairs. She was probably up there in her office working away on the computer. She was doing some writing for the local newspaper and was often on a 'deadline,' which meant she had to have an article finished fast.

"You're late!" she called down.

"A little," I yelled back. "I brought home some … some kids from school." I was going to say "friends," but I really didn't think I could call Marcus a friend. I went to the bottom of the stairs. "Can I get a snack for us?"

"Go ahead. I'll be down as soon as I'm through."

Kia and Marcus followed me into the kitchen. I grabbed some cookies from the cupboard while Kia pulled out three pops from the fridge.

"Maybe we should get started right away on the poem so we can have plenty of time to shoot some hoops," I suggested.

"I brought what I've written so far," Marcus said.

"Great! How far have you got?" I asked.

He rose to his feet and pulled a crumpled piece of paper from his pocket. "Not far. I'm still on the first line."

"That's a start. Let's hear it."

Marcus uncrumpled the paper and cleared his throat. "The basketball is black and orange."

Kia nodded. "That's good. All we have to do is find a rhyme for orange."

"I've been trying for three nights. I can't get it."

"My mother showed me a trick to get rhymes. You get the word, and then start at the beginning of the alphabet and work your way through, writing down every word that rhymes."

"That sounds easy enough," Marcus admitted.

"Okay, let's start. Hmmmm … no 'a' word … borange, corange, dorange … ummm … forange … horange."

"But none of those are actually words, are they?" Kia asked.

"Nope. Keep going," Marcus suggested. "Umm, jorange, korange, lorange —"

"So did you get something to eat?" Mom asked as she came breezing into the kitchen. Her brow furrowed at the sight of Marcus.

"I see we have a new guest in the house."

"Mom, this is Marcus … Marcus Bennett."

She came forward and offered her hand to shake.

"It's nice to meet you, Marcus. Any friend of Nick's is always welcome here."

Marcus just nodded his head.

"You must be the biggest grade three in the school," she said.

"I guess I would be, if I was in grade three. I'm a fiver."

"Grade five?"

"Yeah," I broke in. "Marcus is on our team for the three-on-three tournament. I told you before."

"I'm sure you did. You know how it is, though. Sometimes when you go on about basketball, I stop paying attention."

Mom liked sports okay, but she sometimes thought that both Dad and I spent too much time on them.

"And I guess the contest is being run by that *wonderfully* dressed Mr. Roberts," she continued. Mom was active on the parents' council and was often at the school.

"Come on, Mom, he's the gym teacher. He's supposed to dress in sweats."

"That's a matter of opinion. I think teachers should all dress more formally. When I went to school, all the male teachers wore jackets and ties."

I thought it was best to change the subject. "We're finishing up our poems."

"I thought you and Kia finished last week."

"We're just giving Marcus a hand with the finishing touches on his," Kia said.

"But we're having trouble. Can we use the rhyming dictionary? We need to find a word that rhymes with orange."

"Orange!" she chuckled. "Even that dictionary won't help you. Nothing rhymes with orange."

"Something must," I argued.

"Nothing. A rhyme for orange doesn't exist. You'll have to try something else. Why don't you all go up to my office? The rhyming dictionary is on the shelf. There's plenty of paper and you can work undisturbed. I was just going to bake a batch of muffins. I'll bring you up some when they're ready."

We headed out of the room.

"Marcus?" my mother called out and we stopped.

"I heard a new family with a son about your age just moved in over on Hudson. Is that your house?"

"Nope. Me and my father live over on Maple."

"Maple?"

"Yeah, in the complex."

"Oh ... the complex ... I see."

I couldn't put my finger on it, but somehow her voice seemed a little bit different.

Chapter 8
Done Like Dinner

"Almost finished?" Mom asked. She was standing in the doorway. This was the fourth time she'd been up; twice to bring us food, and once to tell Kia she had to go home for supper.

"We just finished," I answered. "And it's really good."

"It's all right," Marcus said quietly.

"Do you want to read it, Mom?"

"Could you read it to me? I seem to have misplaced my glasses again."

Marcus and I exchanged a look and a chuckle.

"What's so funny?" Mom asked.

I pointed to the top of her head where her glasses were perched.

"Oh, thank you," she mumbled as she pulled them down. "Sometimes I get so distracted when I'm on deadline, I lose track of things. Why don't you read it to me anyway? Poetry is meant to be said more than it is to be read."

Marcus didn't look comfortable with that idea.

"You don't have to if you don't want to," I offered.

"That's okay, I guess." He cleared his throat and began.

> *"The ball moves like it's on a string,*
> *Dancing, jiving, I can make it sing,*
> *Opponents try to take it away,*
> *I make my move, a difficult play,*
> *I pass the ball and drive the hoop,*
> *A pass comes back, a perfect loop,*
> *An alley-oop for two!*
> *We win!"*

"What do you think, Mom?"

"I think, that if Marcus plays basketball as well as he writes poetry, then your team is going to win for sure."

Marcus burst into a gigantic grin, and I realized it was the first time I'd seen him smile — not just today, but ever.

"It's time for your friend to head home. Our supper is ready."

"Couldn't we shoot some hoops first? Dad isn't even home yet, is he?"

"He called and said he had to work late."

"Again? What does that make ... three times this week?"

"Four," Mom said. "But it's not his fault. He's got that big project and the work has to be done and you know he'd —"

"— be home if he could," I said, finishing the sentence I'd heard a lot more than once over the past two months. It was a good thing I had a picture of my father on top of my dresser. Otherwise there was a danger I'd forget what he looked like.

"So it's just the two of us for dinner tonight."

"Could Marcus stay for supper?" I asked.

"His meal is probably almost ready as well," Mom replied.

Marcus shrugged. "Nope. It only gets ready when I get home."

"That's very considerate of your parents to wait like that," Mom commented.

"Marcus fixes his own suppers."

"He does?"

"Not every night. Only when my father works twelve-hour shifts like this week. He makes the chow when he's home."

"And does your mother work long shifts as well?"

"I don't know," Marcus said. "She doesn't live with us."

"I see." Her tone of voice and expression seemed different again.

"So can he stay? I know we have enough since Dad isn't here."

"I'm not even sure your friend would like what I've made."

I inhaled deeply and recognized the

aroma. "Everybody loves lasagna," I protested.

"It sure smells good," Marcus said.

"Then I guess it's all right. Why don't you call home to ask permission ... " She stopped, remembering there was nobody there to ask.

"Nice shot!" I exclaimed as Marcus made a left hook shot. He nodded his head and a hint of a smile curved up the sides of his mouth.

Things were a lot more comfortable out here on the driveway than they'd been at the dinner table. Marcus liked my mom's cooking, which always made her happy, but he didn't have very good manners. He didn't burp or talk with his mouth full or anything, but he didn't say please or thank you, and he held his knife like it was a weapon, stabbing at the food instead of cutting it up the right way.

Marcus tossed up another shot. It circled the rim before dropping through the mesh.

"That's game," Marcus said.

"Do you want to try another one?" I asked.

He shook his head. "I've got to get going. If I'm not there when my father gets home, he gets worried. I'd better get my backpack."

I took the ball and rolled it onto the grass. We'd played four games of one-on-one and he'd beaten me all four times. The last game had been a little closer than the others, but I couldn't help thinking he'd taken it easy on me. He was good — very good.

Marcus followed me back into the house. His backpack was hanging on a hook just inside the door.

Mom popped her head around the corner. "Oh, I thought it was your father," she said, sounding disappointed.

"Marcus has to get home."

"My father will probably be home soon," Marcus said.

"Hopefully Nick's father will be home before too long as well," Mom commented.

Marcus slipped his backpack over one shoulder. He was just getting ready to leave when he paused at the door.

"That was about the best meal I've had in a long time … thanks for feeding me."

"It was my pleasure, Marcus," Mom said.

"See you tomorrow, Nick."

"Don't forget to hand in your poem. You have it, right?"

"Right here," he said, patting the backpack.

"Marcus," Mom said, "please give us a call when you get home."

"Call you?" he asked, sounding puzzled.

"So we know you got home safely," she explained.

"I'll be fine."

"I'm sure you will, but please call so I know."

"It'll make my mother stop worrying," I said.

"Okay … I guess I can do that."

Chapter 9
Winning Ugly

"That stunk!" Marcus pushed through the double doors of the gym. We rushed out after him.

"Well, we won," Kia said.

"We beat them eighteen to six," I added.

"We won ugly!" Marcus complained. "We should have been able to walk all over them. What was with your shooting?"

I'd only put the ball up twice all game and neither of them had dropped. Sometimes, when I missed my first shot, I was nervous about taking the second.

"Yeah, you were really off," Kia said.

"You should talk!" Marcus said, pointing a finger at her. "What did you get, one basket?"

"One two-pointer and a foul shot."

"Three points," Marcus barked. "Congratulations. I have to get to class."

"Maybe if you and Kia come over to my place after school we can practice," I suggested.

"*We* don't need to practice," he snapped. You two do." Then he turned around and stomped off.

"I guess we didn't play that well," I admitted.

The gym door opened and a bunch of kids came pouring out, including the three guys we'd just beaten — two grade-four kids and one guy in grade five. A lot of teachers, including Mrs. Orr, had also been watching. As kids continued to file out, Roy came through the doors. He was on a team with Kingsley and a boy named Dean, who was in grade four. They had won their first game twenty-six to nothing. They hadn't won pretty either.

Roy stopped right in front of me and put his hands around his neck like he was choking himself. He'd been doing that every chance he could since he'd found out Marcus was on my team. I couldn't tell if he was trying to tell me that I was going to choke when we played them, or that he actually wanted to choke me. I tried not to get close enough to find out.

The bell rang and everyone left for class. Kia and I rushed off too. I really didn't mind going to class this afternoon. I had to finish up my story about what I wanted to be when I grew up — of course that was an NBA player. Then I'd go to the library and log onto the Internet. My job was to go on the Julius Johnson web site and find out everything there was to know about him. The hardest part for me would be finding something that I didn't already know.

"You and Kia played a good game," Mrs. Orr said as we entered the room.

"We didn't play a good game at all."

Kia shook her head in agreement.

"I may not know all that much about basketball, but isn't scoring more points than the other team considered a good thing?"

"We won, but we won ugly," I explained, using Marcus' term. "I played bad."

"Well, Nicholas," she replied, "you didn't score as many points as you usually do when you play."

"Yeah, I usually get … how did you know that?"

"Who do you think reads the journal entries you've been making for the last three months?" She chuckled. "Didn't you once score twenty-two points in a game?"

"Yeah, I did … but that was against kids my age. I guess it's different playing with older kids."

"It is," Kia added. "They're older and bigger and taller."

"It's true they are older, but I really didn't notice much difference in size. You and Nicholas are both fairly big for your age, and Kia, you were taller than two of those boys on the other team."

I had noticed that before the game when I was sizing up our opponents. They weren't that much bigger than us.

"Just remember the important thing isn't winning, but being a good sport and ... Rebecca, Sarah, Jessica — get your books out, and stop talking! Everybody get down to work!"

"Ready to go?"

I turned around. Marcus was standing there with his backpack slung over his shoulder.

"Are we going to my place?" I asked.

"That was the plan. Is Kia coming over?"

I nodded.

"Then let's get going. Judging by how we played today, we can't afford to waste any more time."

Chapter 10
Personal Foul

A shrill whistle signaled the end of the game — twenty-three to three for us!

"Good game, Nick and Kia," Deidre congratulated us.

"Thanks," I said. "You and Nandinie and Kyle played a good game too."

Nandinie laughed. "Yeah, right, really good ... that's why it was so close."

"Okay, everybody!" Mr. Roberts yelled. "Hurry up. It's time to go home!"

I sat down on the bench beside Kia

to change shoes. My Dad had bought me a new pair especially for the tournament, and I had to promise him I'd only wear them in the gym.

"Where's Marcus?" Kia asked.

"He had to head back to his class. He said he forgot his math homework and that he'd meet us by the swings."

"We played better today. I guess all our practice is paying off," Kia observed.

"Beating those three didn't have much to do with practice. We're just better than them."

The three of us had been practicing though — every day after school at my place. Marcus had even stayed for supper two more times. My mother seemed to overlook his table manners because he liked her cooking so much.

One night Marcus had stayed a bit later and my father came home before he left. They talked a little bit of ball and then the three of us played some pickup on the driveway. After that my Dad drove him home. On the way back he told me he thought Marcus was a good guy.

"How many points did you get in that game?" Kia asked.

"Ten. You got ten too, didn't you?"

"Yeah. Marcus only popped in three points," Kia said.

"He made some great passes. When you get the ball in your hand and you're that open, it's easy to score."

Kia nodded. "Easy is good. That makes four wins in a row. I looked at the standings, and I think we're in the playoffs even if we lose our last game."

"That's good to know … not that we're going to lose or anything."

We finished loading our backpacks and left the now deserted gym. The halls were empty as well. The sound of our steps echoed off the walls. We left through the side doors and heard them click shut behind us, locking us out. We turned the corner of the school, and there was Roy and a few other kids on the swings.

"Oh, great," Kia said. "Do you think we should keep walking?"

"We can't. We have to wait for Marcus."

"Then let's just stand over by the school and maybe Roy'll leave us alone."

"Yeah, right," I said. "I ran into him in the washroom yesterday and he kept talking about flushing me down the toilet."

"Did he touch you, or was it all talk?"

"Talk. I heard he's been told he'll be suspended for two weeks if he gets into another fight."

We sat down with our backs against the school wall. Without looking directly at the swings, I kept an eye on Roy. He was swinging back and forth.

"Hey, Nick!" he screamed and I looked over.

He took one hand off the rope and slipped it around his neck. Then he laughed, jumped off the swing and came toward us. I swallowed hard.

He stopped directly in front of Kia and me, towering over us.

"Wait for the real games to start," Roy snarled. "Sooner or later you're going to have to play my team and then, bang!"

he shouted, punching his fist into the palm of the other hand. "You two shouldn't even think you have a chance of beating us. I'm not a good loser, so you'd better hope I don't lose."

Neither of us answered. I looked over at Kia. She looked as scared as I felt.

Roy smirked. "Even fancy new basketball shoes aren't going to help you. Why aren't you wearing your pretty new shoes?"

"They're in my backpack," I mumbled.

He reached down and snatched my backpack.

"Hey, don't do that!" I protested, rising to my feet.

"I'm just looking," he said. He undid the buckle, pulled out one of my shoes and tossed the pack to me.

"Fine-looking shoe ... really light ... it practically flies out of my hands." He tossed it a couple of feet into the air and caught it. He tossed it again, this time even higher, and caught it once more.

"Boy, these shoes are so light they might just take right off into the air." He gave a sick little smile. "It would be a shame if they flew so high they ended up on the roof of the school."

I watched as he tossed it again. The shoe soared up into the air, bounced off the wall close to the top, then began to fall down again. Just as it reached Roy's hand, it was snatched away by Marcus.

"These shoes are too small for you," Marcus said.

He handed me the shoe and I quickly stuffed it back into my pack. Roy took a step toward Marcus, stopping only a few inches away. They stood there, silently, just staring at each other.

"Excuse me," Kingsley said as he slipped in between the two of them. They both backed up slightly. "Are the two of you forgetting? If Ms. Grieve hears about a fight, you'll both be gone from the tournament."

Both looked like they were thinking his words over, but neither moved.

"How about you settle it later ... on the court?" Kingsley suggested.

Both Roy and Marcus remained frozen like statues.

"Is there a problem here?" We turned to see Mrs. Jackson standing on the step of her portable.

"No, ma'am ...," Kingsley said, smiling. "We'll all just heading home. Come on, Roy," he added, taking him by the arm and leading him away.

Roy turned back around as he was walking. "See you later, chumps!"

Chapter 11
New Math

It had been a terrible day. At lunch we'd played our fifth game. This time we didn't win ugly — we lost ugly. The other team was okay, but we made them look great. Two of them were in grade five and one was in four. They had height on us and they kept passing the ball until they got a clear shot. If they missed the shot, they muscled us out for the rebound. When we got the ball, they doubled down on Marcus. When we tried to feed him the ball, they kept picking off our passes.

But we still qualified for the playoffs the next day.

I'd been staring at my book all through silent reading, but I hadn't turned a single page. The words kept on blurring with my thoughts.

A book slapped down on my desk. I was so startled I jumped slightly. I looked up at Camilla, who was standing there smiling. She was handing back our journals. The book was open to the entry I'd made right after lunch. I'd written about how bad I felt about losing the game. In red ink at the bottom of the page was Mrs. Orr's response.

Nicholas,

Sorry you lost your game. You know sometimes 1+1+1 is less than 3. Hope you do better tomorrow.

Mrs. Orr

What did that mean? That didn't make any sense at all …

My thought was interrupted by the bell

signaling the end of the day.

"Don't forget we have a spelling test tomorrow," Mrs. Orr said. "Please put up your chairs and you are all dismissed."

The room erupted with the sounds of scraping chairs, conversation and laughter. I stayed in my seat, looking at the response in my journal.

"Did you get a detention when I wasn't looking?" Kia asked.

"No, I just wanted to ask Mrs. Orr a question. Why don't you go and meet Marcus. I'll be there in a few minutes."

"Okay, but don't be too long. We really do need to practice."

I nodded. She had no argument from me there. Kia left and I put my chair up on the desk. I wanted to wait until all the other kids had gone. Slowly I walked over to Mrs. Orr's desk. She was marking, putting little stars in the books that were well-done. I knew I would be 'starless' when she got to my work. I cleared my throat.

She looked up and gave me a puzzled look.

"I was just wondering ... I don't understand what you wrote in my journal ... you know ... that one plus one plus one was less than three."

"I thought that might be a little confusing. But I'm sure you can figure it out if you think about it."

"I have ... and I can't."

"Maybe you have to try harder. Or maybe you should let Kia have a look at it and then have Marcus try to figure it out." She paused. "Or maybe it will only make sense when you all look at it together."

Her words hit me in the head like a basketball bashed into my brain. I laughed out loud.

"Do you understand now?" she asked.

I nodded. "You're saying that three people all working by themselves aren't the same as three people working as a team."

She smiled. "I knew you would get it. What you three need to do is work as a team. Rotate the ball, get more movement, maybe a few more give-and-go plays."

"Rotate the ball ... give-and-go plays?"

I asked in amazement.

"You don't agree?"

"No, that sounds good. I was just wondering — where did you learn so much about basketball?"

"I've had some very good teachers," she answered. "People who know the game well."

"You have? Who?"

"For starters ... you."

"Me?"

"Yes, you and Kia and the other students in the class — all those stories, journal entries, assignments. And more than half of what I read these days has to do with basketball. A good teacher is also a good pupil and learns from her students. Understand?"

"I do. I'd better get going. We have some practicing to do."

"You certainly do, but don't forget your other practice either," Mrs. Orr said.

"Other practice? What other practice?"

"Your spelling test."

"Could I have more milk?" Marcus asked.

My mother raised a corner of one eyebrow.

"I mean, could I please have more milk?"

Mom smiled and filled his glass to the top.

"That was some practice," I said, changing the subject completely. I hated when she corrected any of my friends' manners, although Marcus didn't seem to mind.

"We were good … very good. Much better than before," Marcus agreed.

"What made this one any different than the other practices?" Mom asked.

"We finally figured out how to play as a team instead of three players. Kia and me were standing around and watching too much — "

"And I was trying to do too much," Marcus said.

"Now we're going to play smart. I'm going to carry the ball more, Marcus is going to drive the hoop and if he takes two men with him, I'm going to dish off to Kia for a short jumper."

"And if she misses the shot," Marcus said, "I'm in good position to box them out and take it off the glass."

"The glass?" mom asked.

"The backboard," I explained. "You know, get the rebound."

Marcus continued. "Some of the bigger kids can muscle Nick or Kia away from the boards, but not me. I can either put it right back up or rotate it back outside for Nick to try a three-pointer."

Mom nodded her head. "That does sound like a plan."

"And tomorrow we'll find out if it's a good plan. The first playoff game is at morning recess. If we win that, we play at lunch. And if we win *that* game, we play the finals after school."

"So you'll be home a little late after school tomorrow," Mom said.

"If we get to the finals," I said.

Mom smiled and reached across the table, placing one of her hands on my arm and the other hand on Marcus' arm. "I'll expect all three of you a bit later. I'll make some muffins to celebrate the victory."

"Could they be chocolate chip … please?" Marcus asked.

"They certainly could be."

She got up and started clearing away the dishes. Marcus and I got up and helped. Just as we were almost finished, Marcus looked up at the time.

"I'd better get going. Thanks for feeding me. I'll call when I get home so you don't worry."

"See you tomorrow," I said as Marcus went to get his stuff and left.

Mom wiped the stove while I finished drying the last of the dishes.

"So tomorrow is the end of the tournament," Mom said.

"Sudden death. It's all over."

"Does that mean Marcus won't be coming over anymore?" she asked.

"Well … we won't need to practice any more … but I don't know. I've kind of liked having him around. Is it okay if he still comes over sometimes?"

"I think that would be okay. Not every

night, but sometimes. It's good to have somebody here who likes my cooking."

"I like your cooking! It's just I like other things better, like Chinese food and tacos and pizza ... Pizza! That reminds me, tomorrow is pizza day. Can I have an extra dollar to buy chocolate milk and a giant cookie?"

"No problem. You finish up and I'll go and get the money."

After drying the last of the dishes, I carefully stacked them on the counter.

I hadn't really been thinking about it much, but I was going to miss having Marcus around when the tournament ended. I was glad Mom didn't have any problems with me hanging around with a fiver. But once this was over, I wasn't sure he'd want to hang with a couple of grade three kids.

"Nick ... "

I turned around. Mom was in the doorway, holding her purse. She looked upset.

"My wallet ... my wallet is gone."

Chapter 12
????

"What do you mean, it's gone?" I asked.

"It's gone. It's not in my purse. The zipper was open and my wallet wasn't there."

"It has to be there," I said, returning to the dishes. Her losing something was no big deal. It happened all the time.

"It's not." Mom dumped her purse out onto the table. An amazing amount of stuff spread out across the table. But her wallet wasn't among the stuff.

"Maybe it fell out and is by the shoes

or ... "

"I looked. It isn't on the floor."

"Then it's probably lying around the house somewhere. You know how you always forget where you put things. I don't know how many times you've lost your glasses."

"Glasses are different," she said.

"How about keys? Doesn't Dad say he'd trust you with his life but not his keys?"

"That's different too. Do you ever remember me misplacing my wallet?"

I had to admit I didn't.

"I always know where it is. I had it earlier today and I always make a point of putting it right back in my purse."

"It'll turn up. It's not like it could walk away," I laughed.

"Maybe it couldn't. But maybe somebody could walk away with it."

I stopped and turned around. "What do you mean?"

"I mean somebody could have taken it."

"Somebody? What somebody? The only people here were you, me, Kia and Mar —" I let the sentence trail off. "You don't think Marcus did it, do you?" I demanded.

"I'm not saying he did. But I know it wasn't me or you. We've known Kia and her family for five years. You've only known Marcus a few weeks."

"Marcus wouldn't take your wallet!"

"And when he left, he would have been right there by my purse, by himself."

"Marcus wouldn't do it!"

"And you don't know about things … money may be tight at his place … maybe he doesn't get an allowance. It's my fault really for leaving it where he could be tempted …"

"You're right!" I yelled. "It *is* your fault! Your fault for blaming somebody without having any proof. I know Marcus and I know he wouldn't do it!" I ran from the room.

"Nick, are you still awake?" It was Dad.

I turned over as he sat on the edge of my bed. I gave him a hug.

"You're home pretty late, tonight, aren't you?" I asked.

"Later than I wanted to be. It's also pretty late for you to be awake."

"I guess so." I hadn't been able to get to sleep. I was feeling nervous about the games tomorrow. More than that, I was still upset about what Mom had said about Marcus.

"I spoke to your mom. She's sorry for blaming your friend without having proof."

"She should be!" I said defiantly.

"But you have to remember that she might be right," he said.

"How can you say that?" I protested. "He didn't take the wallet!"

"I didn't say he did," Dad said. "I just wish it hadn't happened the night before the playoffs. You can't play your best unless you've had enough rest. You don't do well when you don't get enough sleep."

He was right about that. I didn't like to admit it, but I wimped out when I was tired.

"So your mom and I agreed that we won't worry about it at all right now. Let's just let things cool off for a few days."

"What do you mean 'cool off'?" I asked.

"I'm going to help your mom search the house from top to bottom."

"That's what she should have done in the first place before blaming people," I said. "Can you come tomorrow and see me play?"

"There's no place else I'd rather be … but I can't. I've got an important meeting that I can't miss. You can tell me all about it at supper."

"Hah! What makes you think you'll even be home for supper?" I asked.

"All I can do is try." He paused. "And for right now I don't want Marcus to come over to the house."

"But … but, Mom invited him over after school tomorrow."

"He won't be able to come."

"What am I supposed to say to him?"

"You're not going to say anything Nick. Your mom is going to drop into the school at the end of the day to either watch you in the finals or to pick you up. She'll just tell him you've got someplace you have to go."

"So she's going to lie to him?"

He didn't answer.

"That's not much better than stealing," I said. I flipped over, turning my back to my father.

"Nick …"

I pulled the covers over my head.

"Nick . . . I know this hasn't been easy. It's not easy for us either. Just try to get to sleep and I'll see you tomorrow."

"If you get home before I have to go to bed," I said through the covers.

There was no answer. I felt a hand on my shoulder for a second, and then the bed groaned as he got up. I heard him walk out of the room.

If I was having trouble sleeping before my father came in, now it was going to be impossible.

Chapter 13
And Then There Were Two

"Okay," Marcus said, "this is going to be no sweat. We just have to play the same way we did this morning in our first game."

Kia grinned. "Yeah, we were awesome."

"Nick, try to be a little quicker on the in-bounds pass, okay? Okay, Nick?"

"What?"

"The in-bounds pass," Marcus repeated. "Get it in quicker, okay?"

"Sure, no problem ... quicker in-bounds."

"Wake up, will you? This is important,

and you look like you need a nap."

"I didn't get much sleep last night."

"I'm always charged before a big game. I didn't sleep so well either last night, so I know what you mean."

Actually he had no idea why I had so much trouble getting to sleep.

Mr. Roberts blew his whistle to signal the end of the other game. Kingsley and Roy's team had easily won. They were now in the finals and would play against the winner of our next game. Kingsley had been hot outside. Roy had eaten up everything that missed off the boards. He wasn't that good a rebounder, but it looked like the other team was afraid to go under the net against him.

"Let's go," Mr. Roberts bellowed. "We have to get the next game started."

There were a few cheers from the kids gathered on the stage to watch. Mrs. Orr was standing off to the side munching on an apple.

Walking onto the court, I sized up our opponents. Of course, like all the other teams in the playoffs, they were older. There were two guys, Bojan and Dustin, and a girl, Sandra. We hadn't played them before, but I'd watched them in a couple of games. The one boy, Bojan, was a great dribbler and Dustin had a good outside shot, but the best player on the team was Sandra. She could shoot, pass and rebound. She was two years older than Kia and a better player, though I hated to admit it.

"Who won the coin toss?" Mr. Roberts asked.

"We did," I answered, raising my hand.

He tossed the ball to me and I walked over to the side to pass it in. I bounced the ball once and saw Marcus break for the hoop.

"Marcus!" I yelled.

All three members of the other team ran to cover him. I softly tossed the ball to Kia, who was completely alone. She turned, aimed and tossed the ball for the net. A perfect swoosh!

Two–nothing.

Mr. Roberts took the ball and gave it to

Dustin, who walked it out of bounds. The three of us dropped back to a zone around the key. I played at the top, farthest away from the basket. It made sense for the other two to be in close — Marcus had more muscle than me and Kia had more height.

Dustin passed it in to Bojan. I moved out to him, but before I could get close, he put up a long shot. It missed the rim completely, hitting the backboard and then bouncing right to Marcus. He turned and fed it out to me. I was standing just beyond the three-point line. Without hesitating I shot. It was short! It hit the front of the rim. Marcus grabbed it, but was immediately surrounded by all three players. He fed it back out to me.

"Shoot it! Shoot it!" he screamed.

I thought for a split second and then launched it. It hit the rim, rolled around, and dropped!

Five–nothing.

A roar went up behind me from the stage. Kia rushed over and gave me a low five.

"Celebrate after the game!" Marcus barked.

I rushed back to the top of the key and waited for them to put it into play. I knew the game had a long way to go, but I also knew it was already over.

★ ★ ★

The whistle blew to signal the end of the game. Marcus offered us a quiet congratulations. We'd all agreed it wasn't 'cool' to rub it in. We shook hands with the other team. It hadn't been close, but it had been a clean game. I sat down to change shoes and catch my breath. Kia and Marcus plopped down beside me.

"Good game," Kingsley said, offering his hand to each of us.

"Thanks."

"I should have figured you three weren't giving it your all before so we couldn't scout you," he said.

"What do you mean?" Marcus asked.

"Don't go and try jiving me anymore. You were just fooling around in those first five games ... saving your best until the playoffs."

"So you think we're better now?" I asked, although the answer was pretty clear.

"For sure," he said. "It's going to be a good game after school. I'm looking forward to it."

"Looking forward to it because you think you're going to win?" Kia asked.

Kingsley smiled. "I hope we're going to win, but I don't know. Either way, it'll be a good game. See you after school."

We watched him walk through the doors, leaving us alone in the gym.

"Do you think we can take them?" Kia asked.

"They're good," Marcus said.

"Yeah, but do you think we can take them?"

"I've seen every game they've played. Dean always takes the in-bounds and passes off to Kingsley. They use Roy under the rim to grab rebounds. I'll be under the rim ... waiting," he said with a smile. "I can handle him, out-rebound him, box

103

him out and score on him ... easy. That means they're going to have to bring somebody off one of you to double up on me. Then, we hit from the outside."

"So you think we can take them," I said.

"If they play the way we've seen them, I don't think we can take them ... I think we can kill them. I'm so sure I can practically taste those chocolate chip muffins your mom is making for us."

Kia whooped with delight. I smiled, but I knew no matter how we did, Marcus wasn't going to be eating any muffins today.

Chapter 14
The Finals

I looked around the gym. The entire stage was covered with kids. The others sat on the steps. Along the sidelines, standing or sitting on benches, were more than half the teachers in the school as well as a few parents. Where was my mom?

I hadn't been able to do school work all afternoon. I kept thinking about what Marcus had said about going back to my place after the game for our 'victory' muffins. I couldn't help but think how much easier it would be if we lost. Then everybody could just go home and nothing more would have to be said.

"You okay, Nick?" Kia asked.

"Sure, no problem. Why?"

"You just looked kind of lost. Are you nervous?"

I shook my head. "Nope. Way past nervous. I'm scared."

"Don't be scared," Marcus interrupted. "There's nothing here to be scared of."

I nodded my head in agreement, but then I caught sight of Roy. I wasn't sure that Marcus was right.

Then my attention was caught by my mother and father walking into the gym! They walked right up to us. I was so surprised to see them both, I forgot I was standing in front of the whole school and gave them both a hug.

"I thought it was more important to be here than at any meeting," my Dad said.

"And I've brought you all something for good luck," Mom added.

"You have? What?"

She opened the bag she was carrying and removed six bright purple, Raptors sweatbands. She handed two to each of us. We mumbled thanks and put them on.

"I was out at the store this afternoon, saw them, just pulled out my *wallet* and bought them," she said.

"Your wallet!"

"Yes. I found it this morning stuffed in a crack in the couch. You were right, Nick, when you said it would turn up. You were right about everything."

She placed a hand on my shoulder.

"These are great sweatbands," Kia said. "I love the Raptors."

"It seemed right to get you Raptors wear — you three are going to eat up the other team."

The shrill blast of the whistle let us know it was time to start.

"Good luck!" she said and reached out and gave me another hug.

"Yeah, good luck," my father said. He reached over and shook my hand, then

Kia's and finally Marcus'. They went and took seats on the sidelines.

"Okay, let's do it," Marcus said. "Just like we planned it."

I walked over and took the ball from Mr. Roberts. He signaled play to start. Kia set up in the middle and, as expected, Dean took up a spot beside her. Marcus broke for the net and Kingsley went with him, leaving Roy to cover me. Roy rushed up right beside me.

"Surprise, you little geek. You're mine," he said.

I held the ball, trying to think of what to do. Roy was supposed to go under the net, the way he had in all the other games. He waved his hands around, trying to block my view. Kingsley was on top of Marcus like a blanket. Kia broke toward me and I sent in a bounce pass. It hit her hands, but glanced off loose and Dean grabbed it. Dean made a quick move and, as Marcus went out to meet him, lobbed it over his head to Kingsley, who laid it up for two quick points.

A wave of cheers washed over us from the stage.

Two more times I put it in and two more times they put it in the net.

"Time-out!" Marcus called out.

"Time-out?" Mr. Roberts questioned. "There aren't any time-outs."

"Umm … I need to tie my shoe," Marcus said.

"It isn't untied," Mr. Roberts said, pointing down at Marcus' feet.

"I'm sorry, did I say tie? I meant I have to take it off because I have something in it."

"Okay, everybody take a short break," Mr. Roberts answered.

Marcus moved over to the bench and motioned for us to follow him. He sat down and slowly took off his shoe.

"This isn't working. We have to make some changes. Do you see what they're doing?" he asked.

"Yeah, they're beating us good," Kia answered.

"They're playing smart. They're keeping

Nick out of the action and playing two on two against me and Kia. We have to turn it back around."

"But how?" I asked.

"I'm going to in-bounds the ball. That'll keep Kingsley away from the hoop. Kia, you stay outside with your man. I want Nick to work on Roy."

"Me on Roy?"

"We've seen you dribble around him. I know if you box him out, you can pull the rebounds away from him. He's only got one thing going for him."

"Size?" I asked.

"No, the fact that you're afraid of his size. As long as you play him hard and aren't afraid of him, his size doesn't mean anything."

"Come on, let's get going!" Mr. Roberts called out.

"Okay, Nick, it's up to you."

We walked back to the court. Mr. Roberts handed the ball to me. I handed it to Marcus and broke for the hoop. Before anybody could react, I was past them.

Marcus lobbed it to me. I laid it up for an easy two points.

The cheer from the crowd was louder than it had been for any of the other points. Above everybody else's voice I could hear my mother scream and my father yell.

Mr. Roberts gave the ball to Kingsley, who took it to the sidelines. Marcus stood in front of him waving his arms like he was about to take off.

Roy set up under the basket and I set up right with him, close enough to tell he had eaten onions at lunch. He pushed against me. I planted my feet, leaned over and shoved back. His face registered shock — he hadn't expected that from me. The pass came in for Roy. I leaped into the air and poked it away. Kia scrambled after it, picked up the loose ball and pushed it outside to Marcus. He faked a drive for the hoop, set, and put the ball up. It dropped in.

I found myself cheering along with the kids on the stage. I felt a shove on

my back and practically staggered over. I turned around. Roy had pushed me, but Mr. Roberts' back was to us. He hadn't seen a thing.

"Keep your distance or things won't end when the game ends," he said so quietly that nobody else could hear him.

I was stunned for a second — and in that second the ball flew over my head to Roy. He put the ball up as I recovered and moved in. The ball bashed heavily off the backboard. I boxed him out to control the rebound. The ball dropped right into my hands. I began to dribble when I was shoved so hard, I tumbled over.

A whistle blew. "Personal foul!" Mr. Roberts called out.

"I didn't even touch him!" Roy bellowed.

"Button it," Mr. Roberts said. "One more word and I'll add a technical foul."

Kingsley grabbed Roy by the arm and pulled him away. Roy continued to mutter under his breath.

"Two shots and your team gets the ball back," Mr. Roberts said.

I stood at the line and took a long, deep breath. The first shot went up and right in — nothing but net.

"Lucky, really lucky!" Roy yelled.

Mr. Roberts threw the ball back to me. I looked at it and then over at Roy.

I smiled. "Who needs luck when you got skill," I said. I put the ball up. It went in, tying the score.

Mr. Roberts took the ball and handed it to Marcus, who was waiting to put it into play. Roy quickly came up beside me. I faked left, spun right and drove for the net. A quick bounce pass hit me in the hands and I put it up. I released the ball and watched it soar up to the net … then I felt a smash to the head. I crumpled to the floor.

"It was an accident! It was an accident!" Roy yelled.

"Are you all right?" Mr. Roberts asked as he bent down over top of me. Marcus and Kia and Kingsley and Dean crowded around.

"I'm … did the basket go in?" I asked.

"Yeah, it went in," Kia answered.

"Then I'm okay," I said, pulling myself to my feet. I looked up at my parents. My mother looked worried and my father angry. He raised a thumb and nodded.

"Points count. Personal foul. One more shot and then you get the ball over," Mr. Roberts called out.

"That's not fair!"

Mr. Roberts pointed a finger at Roy. "One more word or one more foul — you're gone and your team loses. Got it?"

Roy grumbled but didn't answer.

I took the ball and stood at the top of the key to take the free throw. The shot went off the side of the rim and bounced away. Kia took the loose ball and threw it over to Marcus, waiting to put it back into play. Roy rushed right up to my side and pushed in against me.

"No way you're going to win," he snapped.

"That's where you're wrong. We've already won. You're just not smart enough to know it yet."

Marcus dribbled the ball, moving in and out, keeping it out of Kingsley's reach. There were only a few seconds left in the game. Suddenly he snapped the ball in to me. Kingsley rushed over to double-team me and I bounced it back out to Marcus. He pumped once then threw up a beautiful sky rocket. Just as it crashed through the net, the whistle blew and the game was over!

We'd won! We'd won!

Chapter 15
Celebration!

Marcus and Kia and I hugged each other. Then we were practically bowled over by a crush of kids who charged off the stage and slapped us on the back or shook our hands. Kingsley and Dean were right there congratulating us as well, although I couldn't see Roy anywhere. Through the thicket of kids, I caught a glimpse of my parents, off to the side, hugging each other. As the kids filtered out of the gym, my parents came over to offer congratulations.

"I told you you could do it, honey," Mom said as she gave me a big hug.

"All of you did wonderfully," Dad offered.

"I'm so proud of you — all three of you," she added.

Marcus and Kia beamed brightly.

"And I'd like to offer my congratulations ... and to introduce Mrs. Phillips — Roy's mother," she gestured to a woman standing beside her.

"You're Roy's mother?" I asked in disbelief. I didn't figure Roy had a mother. I just thought he was born and raised under a rock.

"Yes. I want to apologize for his behavior. He's had a hard time settling in to the new school."

"The Phillips are the people who moved into that new house on Hudson," Mom said.

"Hudson? You live on Hudson?"

"Yes, the big white house right on the corner of your street."

"My street?" I asked in amazement. "But

I thought Roy lived in the … " I didn't complete the thought.

"In the what?" Mom asked.

"In the … neighborhood."

"Well, he does. Maybe some time you can drop over and you and Roy can play," his mother suggested.

I didn't even know how to handle that one. Marcus, who was standing behind the woman, made a gesture like he was gagging.

"Perhaps sometime," Mom said, "but if you'll excuse us for now, we have a victory celebration to plan." Then she turned back to us. "What do you say if, instead of muffins, we take you three out for dinner? You can choose any place you want to go."

"All right! Fantastic!" Kia screamed.

"But I think we'll all starve to death waiting for these three to decide on one place," my father said. "Since Marcus scored the winning bucket, I think he should get to pick the place where we should eat. Everybody agree?"

Kia and I both nodded.

"Any place that has food is fine with me," Kia said.

"Then it's settled. Marcus, where should we go to eat?"

"Well ... if I get to choose ... I was thinking ... your place."

"My place?" I stared at him.

"If that's okay."

"Of course it's okay," Mom said.

"I was just hoping. Would it be all right if it waited until next week?"

"Next week?" Mom asked.

"My father's on day-shift so he's home for dinner this week. I'm making him a special meal tonight — meatloaf in tomato sauce."

"Meatloaf? Like the meatloaf I made last week?" Mom asked.

"I watched how you made it and I think I can do it," Marcus said.

"Well, I think we can understand you'd want to be with your father tonight. We'll get together next week, if that's okay with everybody."

"Fine with me," Kia said.

"Well, it doesn't work for me," I said.

"Why not?" Kia asked.

"I don't want Marcus to come over to our house for a meal next week."

Everybody fell silent and all eyes were on me.

"I've gotten used to having him around the house, so I was thinking at least two meals next week."

Marcus flashed me a smile. "Especially if one of those meals is lasagna."